About the Authors

Len and I live in the capital of the Highlands in Inverness. We are friends who would meet up in lockdown to discuss ideas for *Black Diamond*. Len came up with character names and the basic foundation for the various chapters and then I would work on writing the book and deciphering Len's writing ideas. Len is dyslexic, therefore, I rewrote his work into a more understandable format. I have not written a book before but could see the story unfold in my mind's eye and then added my own thoughts and ideas.

Black Diamond

Clare Wallace & Leonard A. Hollywood

Black Diamond

Chimera

A CIP catalogue record for this title is
available from the British Library.

ISBN 978 1 915451 03 3

Chimera is an imprint of
Pegasus Elliot Mackenzie Publishers Ltd.
www.pegasuspublishers.com

First Published in 2023

Chimera
Sheraton House Castle Park
Cambridge England

Printed & Bound in Great Britain

Acknowledgements

Thank you to our local voluntary food bank organisation where Len and I met and became friends. If it was not for them we would not have met, as we are both volunteers there. During the lockdown in 2020 we worked on poetry and self-published a book, then the idea of *Black Diamond* was born. Thanks to many of our friends for their support and friendship and lastly thanks to Len for coming up with the initial idea of *Black Diamond*.

Chapter 1

Jason is coming out of one of the card rooms, it's not the one he frequents most of the time. He sees a staircase and starts to climb. At the top there's a woman walking along the corridor with an ornate tray and carefully balanced on it is a teapot with three cups and a sponge cake.

She looks up at him startled. 'Are you lost?'

Smiling, he responds, 'I was until now.'

She blushes and turns away quickly replying , 'Do excuse me', as she starts to open a door in front of her.

At that moment Jason slides his arm around her to open the door. As he does so a young lady quickly opens it from the inside.

She looks up at him wide eyed and exclaims, 'Hello, I'm Zara, would you like to come in and have tea with us?'

Behind her is another identically dressed girls who mutters, 'I'm Lara, we are twins, oh please say yes.'

The lady with the tray looks at the twins astonished and turns to Jason. 'Do excuse the girls, I'm Abbilene.'

Before she can finish her sentence, Jason replies, 'Thank you, I would love to join you all for tea.'

Slightly bemused but secretly smiling, Abbilene asks the twins to set the table by the fire.

They move the table over putting chairs around it so that Jason and Abbilene are sitting facing each other. Abbilene pours the tea for them all as Jason cuts the cake into four pieces. Lara goes to get a cup from her bedroom next door for Jason to use.

Abbilene pours the tea and they all sit around chatting and laughing; the time passes quickly. She looks at the clock on the wall and goes over to the window to close the long heavy drapes, and Jason stands to help her.

The two of them notice a tall distinguished looking gentleman in the grounds of the manor house. There is no mistaking who the gentleman is, Ottis the owner of the house. Abbilene often sees him outside strolling around the grounds.

Tonight, he stands on the bridge, just over six feet tall with deep Mediterranean tanned skin, a strong jawline and rugged good looks.

His hand is on the redwood handrail with its dragon design made of fine steel. He stands looking at the moonlight, its reflection on the water in the pond looks like a woman's body next to a man's, their fingers touching. Six fountains put out a fine spray.

Ottis looks up, admiring the large black diamond-shaped window above the front double door of the house. On either side of the door is a long rectangular clear glass window. One window depicts the silhouette of a woman and the other the silhouette of a man outlined in fine black glass.

He makes no sound as he seems to glide off the bridge then walks across the damp grass into the house, his attire a long dressing gown of black silk with its silver chain belt around his waist. Some of it hangs down his left side, and it swings gently against his leg.

Abbilene and Jason also see Patti, an elegant lady who is standing watching Jason. She is wearing a midnight blue silk bodice, which shows off her light blonde hair, light blue eyes and iridescent pale white skin.

Patti walks slowly but purposely several feet behind Ottis, clearly visible are her stockings and black riding boots with her riding whip and knife tucked down the right side of her boot.

Abbilene feels slightly embarrassed as she closes the drapes on the scene below. Jason looks at her and reassuringly says softly, 'I'm not part of that, I'm here purely to play cards in the card room and for no other reason.' Abbilene smiles at him, feeling lost for words and rather relieved and just a little less embarrassed.

She whispers, 'The view from this corner of the manor house is so beautiful it always takes my breath away, especially when there is a full moon like tonight.' Jason discreetly takes her hand in his for just a moment and gives it a gentle squeeze of reassurance.

Abbilene turns back to the girls. 'OK, you two, off to bed now.' They both look up at Jason pleading.

'Do we have to?'

Abbilene replies, 'It's late so bed. I'll see you both in the morning.'

The girls stand up and go over to give Abbilene a kiss on the cheek then Jason. As they do so Zara whispers to Jason, 'Abbilene really likes you'. Then they run off to their bedroom closing the door behind them, jumping up onto the bed, whispering and giggling.

Abbilene looks at Jason smiling and says, 'You can call me Abbi, short for Abbilene and please excuse the girls, they are just typical teenagers. I was thinking we could have some wine, would you like some?'

He replies, 'Yes please, I would like that very much. I feel very relaxed and happy being here with you, it's as if I have known you all for such a long time and yet we've only just met.'

Jason moves the tea tray and table away to the other side of the room and pushes a two-seater sofa next to the fire and asks her to sit next to him. She pours the wine and asks him all about his family. He talks about his brother and his wife and their two boys and one girl, they live in a stately home near Canterbury.

One thing that saddens him somewhat is the sadness in Abbi's eyes when she explains about the twins. Their mother and father passed away four years ago in a tragic train accident in America and Abbi is their late mother's sister, the girl's aunt and she is now their full-time guardian.

Jason takes a long deep breath thinking he didn't think it possible to love someone at first sight. Everything about her just takes his breath away, he's never felt this way before.

Abbi senses that too, looks at him and says, 'I'll make up-a bed on the sofa for you if you like as it's getting late.' He agrees and moves his hands around her waist, pulling her onto his lap as they melt into each other's arms, lips meeting.

She knew this was the start of something special. She pulls away from him, breathless, stands and moves to get blankets for him, and as he takes them, she gives him another kiss then runs to her room, closing the door and leans against it, the lock snapping shut.

Jason lies under the blankets thinking about her and wondering what will happen next for them both. He can't stop smiling. The answer comes quickly and he can't wait to see her again.

Chapter 2

Ottis and Patti have a busy night ahead of them, they know that those that come tonight ride or drive their own carriages and look after their own horses.

Sahara walks around the bathhouse in white leather and white thigh-high boots with her whip tucked into her right-hand boot, its handle made of oak.

If they want to play, they have to wait, that's the rules. Most know the real thing will come soon enough when Ottis rings his bell of gold, the signal for them to come and eat.

Ottis gets hold of his belt and opens it to reveal his knee length skin-tight black leather breeches.

He takes a glass of champagne from Patti. Without words, they nod and walk into the large drawing room with its candles lit in various coloured glass shades positioned around the room making it look warm and intimate. She knows the very sight of him will make the women about to make his acquaintance for the first time quiver with excitement; his charm and presence is electrifying.

There are four waiters standing holding silver trays of champagne waiting for the guests. They are dressed in cream pants and red waistcoats, and all have on gold and silver slippers.

Ottis and Patti take their place at their table on a small, staged area so that they can look down on the party as they come into the dining room with its table that sits eighteen.

They have another glass of champagne. Excited voices can be heard coming from a large room next door. Each guest receives a flute of champagne to start the evening off as they come forth into the dining room. Sahara, in all her magnificence in front, has led them there from the bathhouse, her dark skin and ravishing good looks envied by many a lady.

Sahara takes her place beside Ottis and Patti, one lady either side of him. They watch as the guests look around the table for their names on black name cards, men's in silver and the ladies' in gold. As they sit in their places, all eyes turn to Ottis as he rings his gold bell and the food is served.

The starter is asparagus with tongue soup followed by salmon with bean sprouts and soft mashed potato, diced with carrot and artichoke with beetroot for colour. The dessert will be served next door.

Ladies sit between two men, now and then a lady's hand slips under the table to a man's inner thigh and beyond. It's a ladies' game, no men can play, the men's hands must stay in sight above the table at all times. On occasion a lady's hand may meet another's, fingers touching, heightening the feeling of anticipation before exploring further. Talk is lively, however, talk about tonight's proceedings is not allowed. The men must not react, the game lasts until the starter is cleared away.

After the meal they leave the table to go into the room where the sweet is being served. On a large table are four naked bodies, two women and two men, all covered in sweet fruits and cream. A woman steps forward and scoops up some cream from between the man's legs and licks greedily, she thinks of tonight and is burning with desire for the real thing that will come when Ottis rings the bell.

The party of diners gorge on the cream and fruit. Ottis rings the bell and their bowls are taken away and more champagne is served.

One of the guests, Mazie, sits enjoying what she is seeing when suddenly a man's hand takes hers and moves her forward. There is another body behind her, she feels strong hands on her hips. The three move into a bedroom with its lights of deep red that cast shadows all around the room, and sensual music is playing softly. All three stop in the doorway and watch.

A naked blindfolded woman with long dark hair is lying on a four-poster bed, hands tied to the hand carved headboard. Her heart is pounding inside her chest with anticipation. The deep purple silk sheet she is lying on compliments her golden tanned skin and long jet-black hair.

The door on the other side of the room opens slowly and two extremely handsome muscular men wearing black eye masks, black leather shorts and black leather gloves lead an equally beautiful naked redhead who is also blindfolded into the room. She has long golden curls that drape down her back and pale skin.

She is slight in build and easily lifted up onto the bed by the men and positioned so that she is sitting astride the dark-haired beauty who wishes she could reach out to feel and touch the person above her. The men take the redhead's hands and ties them gently behind her back with soft lace purple ribbons.

One of the men starts to move his hands up and over the body of the redhead, the leather gloves caressing her skin and fondling her pert breasts. Each nipple swells and hardens, her breathing changing. The other man moves to the lady on the bed and starts to stroke her, moving his hands all over her body, teasing and heightening her sense of arousal just stopping now and then. It's like an exquisite dance as the men slowly move around each lady.

The redhead is lifted up slightly and positioned so that the woman on the bed's face is between her legs and the lady lying on the bed is told to begin to lick the soft flesh of the other woman's inner thighs.

Expecting to feel a hard cock brush across her lips and enter her mouth, further waves of excitement rush through her as she realises it's a woman above her. The blindfold heightens her pleasure as her imagination runs wild with desire; she wonders if the woman is thinking similar thoughts to her.

She licks and sucks greedily, turned on by this newfound experience. She's more than eager to please, her tongue then starts probing further as the woman above moves forward and moans, squatting down further to find just the right spot.

The two men stand back watching the redhead who is about to orgasm. One signals to the other, at that moment one moves forward, and taking hold of the redhead's waist, pulls her backwards off the dark-haired lady. She's still on her knees at the end of the bed facing away from him.

He eases his finger inside her, then another, she gasps begging for more. He peels down his tight black shorts and slowly pushes himself forward. He begins thrusting slowly and rhythmically back and forth.

The other man climbs onto the bed and starts to pleasure the dark-haired lady, all four are moving together rhythmically on the bed. They orgasm simultaneously, shaking and exploding with sheer pleasure and joy.

Mazie feels the rush of sensual pleasure wash over her at the sight in front of her and is led to a chaise longue next to the bed by the man who was behind her and he starts to undress her. He starts by stroking and kissing her neck. her dress drops to the floor.

He's standing behind her, she feels perspiration form on her forehead as her heartbeat quickens. His hands are gentle as they move, exploring her body.

He gently eases down her under garments and begins to play with her, teasing her, stopping just at the moment when she's ready to orgasm. Relentlessly he plays with her, and she gasps begging for more.

He pulls away and slaps her playfully across her backside, she moans, the feeling of ecstasy heightened. Suddenly he plunges himself into her as she climaxes instantly, her juices running down both their legs. They all play together for a while longer before entering a large foam-filled bath next door where the fun then begins all over again.

In another playroom designed to look like a library, two men, Barry and Ezra, are changing and dressing up as schoolgirls, their secret fetish. They have paid like all the other guests for their fantasy to be fulfilled tonight. They love the feeling of frilly pantalettes and lace next to their skin, and they decide that tonight their schoolgirl names will be Ruby and Zoe.

They leave to go upstairs and wander into a bedroom followed in by an older woman. Before they can say a word she bellows, 'You girls have been bad girls today. Nanny will have to spank you both, on your knees now! Lean over the bed.' They obey, holding each other's hands across the bed.

The woman lifts their short skirts to reveal pink frilly pantaloons. She makes a tutting noise then runs her hand across both their backsides, picks up a smooth cane and brings it down with a hard sharp slap on each backside several times. As they try to move, she leans on then and slides her hand inside one of their pantaloons pulling them down and starts to lick and kiss the marks she's made.

They both move round in lighting speed, each one grabbing an arm as they pull her up onto the bed ripping her dress down the middle. She squirms, trying to get up, enjoying the role play, but they are too strong for her and this excites her further. They rip her under garments off as one holds her down, the other one forces her legs apart, mounts her pushing himself into her as hard as he can. As he moves her body responds.

The one holding her is enjoying the scene and can't wait for his turn to explode inside her. Barry comes and lets out a low moan, and as he moves away, Ezra takes his place. He plunges himself inside her, leans over and takes an erect nipple in his mouth, sucking greedily.

Barry wipes himself clean with the woman's hair then gets a bottle of wine from the other side of the room leaving Barry to finish playing.

Coming back over to the bed, Barry passes the wine bottle to Ezra and says to the woman, 'I'm Ruby and this is Zoe, come, have some wine with us Nanny, we'd like you to stay and play some more with us.'

She looks at them both, smiles and drinks some wine. She giggles. 'Ruby, Zoe you are such naughty girls.'

The bottle of wine finished, she slowly falls asleep sliding down the bed. Barry and Ezra look at her, her legs are open invitingly. Barry can't help himself and starts to fondle her breasts. She's not waking, too much wine he thinks.

Ezra moves on top of her, parting her legs even further and starts to fuck hard and deep. He moves off her and Barry takes his place and fucks as hard as he can. After all this could be his last fuck for a while as they are off to India with the army officers after the party tonight, no more dressing up for quite some time.

They have a bath then change into army uniforms leaving their wet towels over good old Nanny and leave smiling and satisfied, not looking back.

As they walk across the bridge, they take a last look at the pond then into the stables. A carriage awaits to take then to their ship leaving for India.

As they get into the carriage, they notice the seats have been made into a bed and are pleasantly surprised to see two young ladies laying seductively on the bed, satin cushions surround them.

The girls have fun with them, it's a long four-hour journey to the harbour. Ottis had decided he couldn't have the boys getting bored as they are such regular customers, and the girls are a parting gift from him.

Ottis is in the stables looking over at the two horses that Barry and Ezra left behind; they belong to him now. In the distance Patti is approaching from the manor house, there is a rather worried look on her face.

He goes back inside and Patti takes Ottis up to the room where the old girl is clearly deceased and wrapped in two towels. On this occasion, one of the games planned and played has clearly gone wrong, perhaps it was too much for the old dear.

They check that no one is about as he carries her down to the ice house and packs her away until he has time to dispose of her body. The nearby pig farm will do the trick. The body will be eaten in no time at all, leaving no trace behind.

They know no one will be looking for her, she has no family, no relations. In time he will take over her townhouse that's situated in town not too far away from his own dwelling.

Chapter 3

Jason wakes to the clock striking seven and gets dressed. Abbi comes into the room and sheepishly gives him a kiss. She turns and looks longingly at him and mutters, 'I'm falling in love with you.'

Jason replies, 'I feel the same, it was love at first sight and I want to ask you something.'

Abbi looks at him as he nervously takes her hand and says, ' I think you and the girls should leave with me as soon as possible and we should marry. I have a large house not too far away. I just know you will all be so happy there, please let me take care of you all.' She blushes, and accepts his proposal with no hesitation.

They spend the morning together, discussing their future plans and enjoying a leisurely breakfast that Abbi has arranged with the housekeeper then enjoy a walk around the grounds of the manor house.

Later that day Abbi asks to meet Ottis in his office privately. As she comes in he looks at her as she sits down opposite him and he thinks there is something different about her. She is radiating with a newfound confidence that he's not seen before, she looks at him and says, ' I need all the papers you have for the twins.'

Ottis replies, 'What's going on, why do you need them?'

Abbi replies, 'Jason, the gentleman that comes to play cards in the card room, has asked for my hand in marriage. I've accepted, therefore. I'll be leaving soon and taking the twins with me. It's best for all of us, a fresh start, it's what the girls need after all the heartache. I can't thank you enough for all you've done for us, I will miss you, but we will be living nearby and will keep in touch and still see you regularly.'

Ottis sits back in his chair, clasps his fingers together, rolling his thumbs around each other, looking at Abbilene thinking he could lose three of his best people. However, perhaps in the long run he could make this work in his favour, so he looks at her and says, 'I'll ask Sahara to look out the paperwork for the twins. So that's it then, are you sure it's the right decision? If not you know my door is always open for you all.'

Abbi looks at him and says, 'I'm so happy, Ottis, but it's time to move on. I'll give my keys to Patti and she can take over the housekeeping and accounting work.' With that, she leaves the office looking back at him smiling, she's so grateful to him for everything he's done for her. She notices the look on his face, it's one of concern at the sudden rash decision that seems to have come out of nowhere.

Abbilene goes upstairs into her room and is surprised to see Jason sitting there with Lara on his right and Zara sat next to him on his left all holding hands talking intently.

The girls had gone to find him and taken him into her room. She tries to look annoyed at them all for being in her room when suddenly Jason stands up, and before she can say a word, lifts her off her feet, giving her a kiss and explains that he was talking to the girls and telling them of their future plans to reassure them both. Any annoyance she felt is dissolved instantly.

There's a knock at the door. It's Patti with a worried look on her face. 'What's going on? What's this I'm hearing about you leaving?'

Abbi replies, 'That's right, Patti, Jason and I are leaving with the girls in the next few days and we're going to get married.'

Patti looks at her with a sad look on her face. 'I'm really going to miss you all, however, I wish you all the best, a new start, how wonderful and just what the girls need.' Abbi asks her to join them in the drawing room downstairs and have tea and cakes with them all to discuss the wedding arrangements. She decides she wants a quiet affair with Ottis and Patti there with them. She's not one for big lavish parties, preferring something intimate and simple.

Ottis arranges for his coachman, Tom, to deliver their belongings to Jason's townhouse and takes them all on a shopping trip for dresses for the wedding and arranges their stay at the bridal suite at the Grand Hotel.

A few days later, Jason and Abbi book into the hotel leaving the girls to relax as they go to the registry office to register and pick up a marriage licence so that they can marry in a few days time. Because of Jason's status, that Abbi is unaware of as Jason is not one to brag, a marriage licence is granted in two days.

The ceremony is a very quiet elegant affair. The girls are to be flower girls and Ottis and Patti witnesses. Lunch will be provided at the hotel.

Ottis had tried to persuade them both to have an elaborate wedding at the Black Diamond, however, the couple politely declined preferring a quiet affair in the nearby hotel.

In the late afternoon of the wedding a beautifully decorated horse and carriage will be awaiting them all to take them to their new home, all arranged by Ottis as part of his wedding gift to them.

In the few years Ottis had known Abbi, he had become very fond of her, treating her like a daughter. She was recommended to him by a family friend to come and work for him as a housekeeper and bookkeeper, and in turn, this would help her out.

He had heard about her looking after her late sister's two children and being in that situation it would be unlikely that she would ever receive a marriage proposal. The thought of her alone with children, destitute and struggling, tore at his heart strings and he welcomed her into his family with open arms.

The wedding day arrives and the ceremony goes without a hitch. It's a perfect day and the sun is shining. Ottis could not be prouder of Abbi, she looks so beautiful and radiant in her wedding dress. He could not be happier for her and wishes the happy couple all the best. He's very fond of Jason and knows he will make a good husband. He's a hard-working, straight talking, honest man with good morals. He's never been interested in the parties at the Black Diamond despite Ottis trying to persuade him to attend, his only interest had been to play cards.

After the lunch, Jason helps Abbi climb into the horse and carriage holding her hand. She has never felt such joy, this has been the best day of her life. A ready-made family and she hopes one day to have children of her own with Jason.

The twins talk excitedly as their carriage pulls up outside Jason's splendid townhouse. It's the first real home Abbilene and the girls have had in a long time.

The house is grand. It has four floors and is like two buildings joined together to make one. It is home to them all from now on. Jason had not explained he had a title, he would explain all that in due course.

The three of them are standing in the reception room looking around at all the grandeur in disbelief when a man comes out of a side room, and on seeing them bows saying, 'Me Lord?'

Jason glances at Abbi and explains. 'This is our butler, Mr Benson. Benson, is your wife in the kitchen?'

Benson replies, 'Yes me Lord.'

Jason replies, 'Right lead the way, let's get the formalities over with.'

A shocked and bewildered Abbi and the girls, whose mouths are hanging open as if to catch flies, follow them into the kitchen where a woman is standing wiping her hands on a tea towel, with two teenage girls by her side cleaning the range.

Jason addresses them, 'Mrs Benson, our cook and Sue and Jackie, her daughters. May I introduce you to my new wife, Abbilene and her two nieces, Zara and Lara. You girls are all of similar age, therefore, you should all get along splendidly.' The shock on their faces seems to equal that of Abbi's and the girls.

'Benson perhaps we could all do with a welcome drink, I propose a sherry for the girls, Abbi and Mrs B and a whisky for you and I, then perhaps Mrs Benson you could show the girls to their rooms and they can choose which ones they want.'

The sherry and whisky poured, Jason announces, 'Benson, Mrs B, girls you must all join us in a toast.' He raises his glass and proudly announces, 'To my beautiful wife and my new family, to all of us, here's to new beginnings.'

Zara asks, 'May we have Sue and Jackie show us around after our drinks please, Mrs B?'

She looks up at her girls. 'Go and show the twins their rooms, the ones with the bathroom between them, let me know that you are happy with the room choices.'

The four girls rush excitedly up to the bedrooms and Sue and Jackie take their bags up for them and leave Lara and Zara in their rooms to settle in.

Lara notices a large wooden trunk at the end of her bed, opens it and slams the lid shut. She runs into Zara's room. 'Zara, come quickly, look what I've found.'

They open the trunk together and in disbelief shut it again, Zara looks at Lara. 'I think we had better tell Abbi.' The two girls go downstairs to find Abbi standing at the bottom of the stairs sorting out her luggage.

She looks up. 'Are you OK girls? What's the matter?' She can tell by their faces that something is very wrong.

Zara takes a deep breath. 'Abbi please come with us, we've found something very odd.' She follows them up to Lara's room and points at the trunk. Abbi opens it and looks inside. A substantial amount of money is lying underneath a riding whip and below that an assortment of under garments that a lady would certainly not wear. It was most out of place in a house such as this and would be more at home in the Black Diamond.

Abbi takes the money and puts it to one side, deciding she will put it in the office later for safe keeping.

She puts the rest of the items back into the trunk and slams the lid shut. With that Sue enters the bedroom. Abbi turns to her. 'Sue could you please find your father and Jason and ask them to come up here now please.' She had a look of utter disgust and annoyance on her face.

Jason and Benson come up the stairs and into the bedroom and Jason addresses Abbi. 'What's wrong my love?'

Abbi points at the trunk. 'I don't know what's been going on here but can you please both carry that trunk downstairs. I do not want it near my girls and then perhaps as explanation of its contents would be in order. Please do not open it now, just get it out of my sight.' She can feel the anger bubbling up inside her.

Jason looks at Abbi, astonished. 'I know nothing about the trunk, my darling, and of course we will get it moved right away.' The two men get hold of each end of the trunk, it's heavy and they struggle down the stairs leaving it outside the office.

Benson looks at Jason. 'Boy that wife of yours has some temper, what on earth has got her so upset?' With that they open the trunk and realisation hits them both.

Jason replies, 'My Abbilene is from Texas, she's a feisty one, that's part of what I love about her. I don't know how I am going to explain this. Benson, can you come back upstairs with me, let's see if she's calmed down.'

The two walk back into Lara's room, Abbi is standing by the window. She turns to them both. 'Would you be able to buy or make a bookcase for each room and a desk and chair as the girls still have two years at school. I would like them to be able to study in their rooms. Also I would really appreciate it if the beds could be replaced as soon as possible, Can you burn the items in the trunk and I'd like to keep it, as it's solid oak. She feels rather embarrassed and ashamed by her outburst earlier realising it's not Jason's fault.

Benson answers. 'Yes, ma'am, I can look at getting that done for you. This was a room Miss Woods occasionally used, she's away just now visiting her sister, she comes back and forth now and again. She's our housekeeper, we will need to speak to her once she's back to see if she knows anything about the trunk's contents. She has yet to be informed of my lord's new family.

'Miss Woods also does the accounts. I will be going over the books with Mrs B tomorrow morning as we are not sure when Miss Woods will be back. We may need a new housekeeper and possibly someone to look after the books while Miss Woods is away. Then in the afternoon I can get what you require arranged then.'

Abbi replies, 'It's OK, Benson, if Jason is happy I can look at the books myself, if that's OK with you as that's one of my areas of expertise.' With that Jason and Benson agree.

The next day Abbi goes to the office to find the door locked and calls Benson to unlock it. Benson says, 'There is no key, Miss Woods is the only person who holds that key.' Abbi takes a deep breath of frustration and demands that Benson break the lock.

Abbi sorts through paperwork and finds the book of accounts and starts going through them. She notices a locked drawer and asks Benson to force it open. In the drawer is another set of accounts that looks almost identical to the ones Abbi has been working on, however, on studying it closely she discovers there are some discrepancies and the numbers don't add up the way she knows they should. The heading on the book has Mrs B's name on it.

Abbi spends the next few hours studying the books carefully and comparing them then finally the realisation hits her. Miss Wood has clearly been embezzling money from Jason for quite some time. Fifteen hundred pounds in total by the looks of things is missing. She sits back in the chair thinking, "Wait until Jason finds out about this, first of all I'll find out if Benson or Mrs B know anything about it."

Just then the cook comes into the office and Abbi hands the book to Mrs B asking if she has seen it before as it has her name on it. Mrs B replies with a shocked look on her face. 'I've never seen that book of accounts before, Miss Woods deals with all the financial matters of the household and has done for years. I don't get involved with the finances, I don't know why my name is on it.' With that Abbi explains her findings.

Mrs B looks at her astonished. 'We must inform your husband at once, he will need to contact Miss Woods and have words with her. I'm not sure when she will be back. however I don't think he will allow her to continue working here, what with the business with the trunk contents and now this! He'll have her sleeping on a park bench, not residing here.'

Abbi looks at Mrs B. 'Please don't mention to the girls about the contents of the trunk, my girls only just glanced into it and I think it's best if we don't discuss the matter again with them.'

Mrs B says, 'Would you mind if I send your girls and mine out clothes shopping as a distraction from all this upset. Keep them out of the way, while we have a talk about all this with your husband and Benson.'

Abbi replies, 'That's a really good idea, let's go and see the girls now.'

Chapter 4

The four girls come down the stairs, three of them all talking at once. Abbi calls Zara into her office and hands her some rolled up notes and asks her to be in charge of things.

She agrees and is happy to be the one to keep them in check for the forthcoming outing. Mrs B is standing by the front door and Abbilene is stood by the office. All four girls wave to them as they go out of the door towards the carriage that is awaiting them, passing a tall woman in a long skirt and jacket, who has just come out of the carriage.

The woman enters the house, a little bewildered wondering who the girls are with Sue and Jackie. In front of her an unfamiliar woman is standing at the open door of the office and marches in ahead of her and sits down behind the desk pointing to the chair across from her. 'You must be Miss Woods, I would like you to tell me about the books in front of me and don't think of running, it's too late for that. You and I know you are a thief and don't try and lie to me. I have your books, both sets, if it was up to me you would go to prison right now.'

Miss Woods tries to say that one set she has never seen before. Abbi ushers Mrs B to take her away saying, 'I don't care about you or your excuses, money has been going missing for many years and don't try blaming Mrs B, even though her name is on the front of one of the books. You have been stealing long before Mrs B ever started working here, put your keys on the desk then leave this house for good. Your employment is terminated and the authorities will be in touch as this embezzlement will have to be investigated further.'

Abbi stands up and leans against the desk. 'By the way, all the things you had upstairs in that trunk have been burnt.' Turning red with embarrassment, Miss Woods is clearly dumbfounded and unable to speak and looks like she's about to burst into tears. Unaffected by her little charade, Mrs B takes hold of her elbow and escorts her out of the house.

Abbi meets Mrs B as she closes the door on Miss Woods. She says, 'I don't know about you but I need a drink.'

Mrs B looks at Abbi and says, 'Come and have a drink with me in the kitchen before I start work. Let's take our mind off things. I wonder what the girls are doing right now, I hope they are having fun.'

***

Zara and the girls have finished their day out when she glances across the street and sees the Grand Hotel where they stayed prior to their aunt's marriage. She checks what money she has left after their shopping spree and decides that there is enough left to treat the four of them to afternoon tea in the hotel's plush tea room. They go into the tea room and find a table by the window looking onto the high street.

Four waitresses are on duty watching the girls come in. Three stand together whispering, ignoring the other rather plain looking plump waitress. The three of them are looking at the girls with raised eyebrows thinking they are not their normal type of clientele. The one who seems to be in charge sends over the plain looking waitress to take the girls' order.

Two pots of tea and a cream slice each is ordered. Zara keeps an eye on the time to make sure they give themselves enough time to get home in time for dinner, not that they will need much to eat once home.

On asking for the bill, Zara asks for four chocolate eclairs in a box, one each for Jason, Abbi, Benson and Mrs B.

***

Abbi is in the hallway and the doorbell rings. It's the fishmonger at the door delivering the fish order for Mrs B. She takes the fish into Mrs B then decides to go into the library to relax for a while. The doorbell goes again and Mrs B answers. This time, standing in the doorway, is a well-dressed man who hands her an envelope and says, 'For the lady of the house.' And with that he's gone before Mrs B can even reply.

Mrs B calls Abbi and hands her the envelope explaining, 'This has just been hand delivered by a very well-dressed young man.' Abbi opens it and inside is a piece of paper with a black diamond motif on the right-hand top corner and a note saying there is five hundred pounds for each of the girls. There is no indication of who it's from, but she thinks it must be from Ottis. She'll ask him about it later, meanwhile she pops it into her skirt pocket.

Sometime later, there is a commotion at the front door as the four girls come in; they are in high spirits chatting and laughing loudly. Mrs B meets them all in the hallway. 'Stop, one at a time girls, coats off, wash your hands please, then take a seat in the dining room. Dinner won't be long, please keep your voices down as your step father is in the library reading *The Sporting Times.*

***

Miss Woods looks in her purse for the coach fare to her sister's on the coast. After being dismissed from Jason's home, a few days sleeping in the park is enough for her. She wishes she hadn't spent so much on cheap gin to numb the pain she was feeling.

Nearing the coach station, she has the feeling that someone is watching her, the idea of a detective on her tail keeps creeping into her mind. She has to get away, the only place she can think of is her sister's hotel.

Turning a corner, she bumps into two young men that almost knock her over, spilling the contents of what meagre possessions she has onto the pavement. The men seem well dressed and affluent, they apologise and start to pick her items up. With that she bursts into tears, saying someone has stolen her money and that she needs to get to the coast to her sister's hotel.

One of the men explains that they are wine merchants and are on their way to see new customers via the coast road and perhaps they could give her a lift and speak to her sister about possibly supplying her hotel with their wine.

With that thought in mind, Miss Woods agrees grateful for the assistance. She feels instantly relieved, almost elated at the outcome of such a generous offer of help.

She boards the horse and carriage. The men have a driver, therefore, they enter after her into the carriage and sit opposite her. One of the men says, 'My name is Ralph and this is Pierre, would you like a glass of wine, it might steady your nerves after having such a bad experience.'

Miss Woods replies, 'That would be lovely.' One of the men opens a bottle and pours wine into three glasses and hands them round. The wine flows freely for several hours, and slowly, Miss Woods is getting drunk. The men notice her speech starting to slur as she mentions feeling uncomfortably warm inside the carriage.

They help her off with her jacket. She giggles, leaning against Ralph who rubs his hands over her breasts deliberately but pretending it's an accident. Pierre slides his hands up inside her long skirt, she doesn't seem to object or even notice. Ralph turns to face her and kisses her, she doesn't resist as she is eager to please him.

Pierre feels for the soft lace top of her stockings, and takes hold of her pantalettes, pulling them down her legs and off. He opens the carriage window and flings them outside, thinking she won't be needing them any more once she finds out what's in store for her. He begins to explore the mass of dark curls he finds between her legs, fingers probing and searching for the opening between her legs.

They travel into the night changing horses part way through the journey. Miss Woods is too drunk to notice, but finally they reach her sister's hotel. It's late as the men dismount from the carriage.

Ralph and Pierre realise she can't walk unaided due to the effects of the alcohol. They both put an arm around her waist as she puts an arm around each of their shoulders, giggling at all the attention that's being given to her. She points to where they should go, but there is no sign of the sister. No doubt she will be in bed, but the side door is unlocked, so she manages to direct the men to a room that they presume is the bedroom for her to use. Giggling she falls onto the bed.

Miss Woods wakes up with a banging headache. She manages to sit up, and on hearing raised voices outside, looks out of the window. She sees a tall distinguished looking man standing next to a small Asian looking woman who is holding a book and writing something down in it. They are all looking very serious, she can't help but think she should be down there joining her sister and that something sinister is going on.

Looking around the room, she searches for her clothes. All she has on is her lace under bodice that is ripped slightly. Her blouse, skirt, pantalettes and jacket seem to be missing and not in the room. She's trying to remember what happened the night before and can't remember anything of her journey or arriving here. She notices bruises on the tops of her thighs and suddenly feels very concerned, trying to think what that could possibly mean.

She sees a pile of clothes on a chair near the doorway, and picks up the black stockings with red lace tops, a skirt, blouse and under garments, the blouse has no buttons on it, just six pieces of black ribbon. She puts it on and ties it up. The skirt has no buttons either and she thinks this odd, it just has a black cord around the waist. She tries to pull it down a bit,, however it's so short just coming to the top of her stockings and hardly covering her at all.

She's feeling very uncomfortable, confused and wondering where her clothes are and not understanding why these clothes seem to be left out for her. They are not at all the style of clothing she would wear.

She walks out into the garden to her sister who is sitting on a bench looking distraught. Miss Woods addresses her sister, 'Audrey, what the hell is going on, what's wrong, what did those people want and look at me. Whose clothes are these and why were they left out for me, where are my clothes?'

Audrey tries to speak but no words come. Looking up, the man and woman appear in front of them both. The woman steps in front of Miss Woods, looking as her distastefully. 'I'm Low Lin, I'm in charge here now. This is Ottis, I now run this hotel that he will be taking over, you were followed here by two of his men. We know all about the thieving of money from Jason and his family and you belong to me now or will suffer the consequences of the law and jail.'

Audrey comes to the realisation that the money her sister kept giving her to invest in the hotel over the last few years was this stolen money, and now she's implicated too.

Miss Woods tries to step past Low Lin as Ottis stops her in her tracks, grabbing her arm. Low Lin lifts Miss Woods' short skirt and hits her hard across the backside with a fan she's holding, twists her around to face her and pushes the tip of the fan under Miss Woods' chin so that her head snaps back as far as it will go. She grabs hold of her hair in the other hand. 'Did you not hear me, we own you now and you work for us and will do as you are told. Now get back to your room until I call you.'

Miss Woods runs off towards her room, sobbing and not looking back, Ottis has already explained everything to Audrey who knows that they have no choice but to comply. Miss Woods is to become a whore to repay her debts, and the hotel will be converted into a bordello for ladies of the night.

Miss Woods is to wear sky blue clothing that she will hate as she normally always wears dark grey. The debt has to be paid in full, running away would mean life on the streets and that's not an option.

Work will begin as soon as possible to transform the hotel. First the stables will be built, a bathhouse with its two new baths. In the men's will be a large silhouette in tiles on the floor of a naked woman and in the women's will be the large silhouette on the floor of a naked man.

The ladies working there will have their own themed room, their clothing will match the colour of the room, starting with Miss Woods, with sky blue clothing and a sky blue room.

Low Lin orders Miss Woods into the landing outside of her room, and taps her fan on the banister of the stairs yelling, 'Come with me, Woods, I have a surprise for you.' With that, she waves her fan in the air and follows Miss Woods down the stairs directing her into a room next to the study.

In the room there are two women standing by a table with a cover on it. Suddenly Low Lin pushes Miss Woods on to the table and the two women grab her spinning her round, pushing her across the table holding her face down. Miss Woods starts to sob and shake uncontrollably.

Low Lin pulls roughly at her clothes exposing her lower back, washes the area with some sort of alcohol spirit, makes four marks on her skin, then tattoos a four-inch diamond shape in red. Above it she tattoos the word *Woods* in black with a red outline around the name.

That's the only name she will have from now on and will not be referred to by any first name. She now belongs to Ottis until her debt is paid in full then he will sell her on; she will never be free.

Chapter 5

Ottis sits in his new office that was in the hotel and is now well on its way to being a high-class bordello thinking about what he'd overheard earlier about an opium den in a back street bar nearby. That would be a nice little earner to take over if he can get his hands on it. A plan is formulating in his mind.

He summons Low Lin and goes through the details with her. Several hours later she meets him at the door of his office with three other women, Ali, Aditi and Aya. Without words Low Lin nods at Ottis and all five of them leave for the bar.

Ottis with his long coat and hat in hand looks like a very distinguished gentleman, his cane carved in wood with a silver lion's head decorating the top of it in the other hand. The five walk the five minutes to the bar passing several locals who can't help but stare, wondering who these newcomers to the area are, they are very different to the usual types they are used to seeing in the town.

Striding into the bar with an air of arrogance and purpose, Ottis notices the stench of stale odour and it's as run-down inside as it is outside. He looks around and a large fat man is standing behind a bar. There are various other dishevelled looking drunk men at various tables, some with scantily dressed whores sat on their knees, one kneels between a man's legs sucking his cock greedily and completely ignores them entering the bar and carries on oblivious to their presence. Her top is pulled down revealing naked pert breasts that the man is fondling.

Ottis addresses the man at the bar, 'Who owns this pile of shit?'

The man sneers, 'Who's asking?'

Ottis replies, 'Never you mind, fetch me the owner.'

The fat man moves out of the bar area and stands in front of the five of them, hands on his hips puffing his chest out, not looking at all happy with the comments from Ottis. He responds, 'That would be me, who are the tarts you've brought with you, they look like they need a good fucking. Best get them out of here before my men get their hands on them. Or is that what you've come for or perhaps it's you that's looking for a fuck. You look like the kind of man that likes it up the arse, eh boys.' With that the men watching laugh, raising their beer bottles and a couple of them stand up as if getting ready to defend the fat man.

Ottis can feel the fury building up inside of him. His dislike for the man was instantaneous the moment he saw him. He glares at him and turns to Low Lin and nods.

Her arms were folded inside the wide sleeves of her elegant cloak, and she moves her hands out of her sleeves at lightning speed, her fan in one hand with a steel blade poking out of the top of it. She moves towards the man and hits him between the legs with the blade and rips sharply upwards as he tries to move but it's too late. His head lolls forwards as his body jerks and the scream he emits is ear piercing.

Low Lin steps back as he slumps to the floor onto his side, writhing in agony turning onto his back. Low Lin strikes again, slicing the blade across his neck. There is silence now apart from the gurgling sound as blood gushes from the open wound.

Calmly, Ottis thumps his cane on the floor, the men that were standing almost knock their chairs over as they sit down, shocked at the sight before them. All eyes are on Ottis as he bellows ' There's a boat round the side, who owns it?'

One of the men points at a woman and says, 'She does.' The woman looks up with a terrified look on her face.

Ottis points to the dead man on the floor and directs his conversation to the woman saying, 'I want that pile of shit moved, tether a weight to his arms and legs and dispose of him. I'll pay you good money to do it.'

The woman stammers, 'My man owns the boat and he'll do it.'

Ottis responds, 'Deal. I'm leaving two of my women here to take charge, my people will be back to clean this shit hole up, I'm taking over this place.'

With that Ottis and Low Lin turn and walk out of the door, leaving two other women in the bar. There are a row of three cottages attached to the bar and they head towards the entrance of the one nearest them.

Walking up the path there's smoke coming out of the chimneys. Ottis knocks on the door, an old man appears in front of him and looks Ottis up and down noticing his fine clothing, thinking he must be some sort of royalty. He feels embarrassed by his own appearance, he looks like a tramp in comparison.

'I'm here on a business matter, pray tell, who owns these cottages? I am looking to buy all of them.'

The old man stands back allowing the two of them to enter. Looking around, it's cold and damp inside despite the small fire burning. A woman is sat by the fire trying to get warm, next to her are two girls, one looks about twelve and the other about fifteen. They look malnourished, their clothing is dirty but underneath the grime on their faces he thinks they are probably quite pretty. The man offers them stools to sit on. Ottis declines, asking the question again.

The old man replies, 'Bill who owns the bar owns these cottages, he's a nasty piece of work, not well liked. We all rent them from him, rips us off he does, leaving us to near starve to death as he takes all our money.'

Ottis asks, 'Who lives in the other two cottages?'

The old man responds, 'Next door is empty and used by the owner, we are not sure for what, and in the end cottage there is a family, a mother with two young girls and a young boy. No one is sure where the father is, people suspect they are Bill's children, if they are, he doesn't treat them very well. All people ever hear coming from that cottage is crying and on various occasions shouting and screaming.'

Ottis thinks to himself that the mother sat by the fire is obviously younger than the old man and would make a good housekeeper and the two girls, given time and the right training, could be just right for fun and games at the Black Diamond.

Young blood is needed to keep the clientele happy, perhaps the girls and mother in the third cottage would also suit him nicely for his growing Diamond Empire. The bar and cottages will be an extension of the recently acquired hotel to be renamed the Red Diamond, and the addition the bar and cottages would make an opium den for the amusement of his guests.

Back in the office of the hotel, Ottis sits ordering more wine and opium to be delivered by boats. Work at the once run-down hotel had been underway for some time, and with the owner of the bar and cottages taken care of and word travelling fast of his demise, the residents of the cottages soon comply with any demands put upon them. Money and food being the main factor in persuading them to enter into a more lavish lifestyle.

Gone were the rags that they wore, food was now plentiful and they were all well looked after.

Ottis arranges for all the people in the cottages to be moved to the Black Diamond for a few months while the building that is to be the Red Diamond is transformed and work on the cottages gets underway. The mother of the children is trained up to be the housekeeper and her children trained to cook and clean, the old man in the other cottage works in the stables. Once fully up to speed their skills will be transferred to the Red Diamond.

Several playrooms were already open and in operation in the Red Diamond. In one of the bathhouses, three women were standing over a man lying in one of the smaller bath tubs, taps at one end, big enough for him to lie in and the three women are standing above him, one leg either side of his naked body.

They take it in turn to urinate over him, something he pays a large sum for. A brunette is standing above his head, giggles and aims for his open mouth, his cock rigid and standing to attention with the anticipation.

A petite blonde, squats down on his engorged cock, her back facing away from him, she doesn't want to waste the opportunity. He reaches for her buttocks, prising her perfectly rounded bum cheeks apart and inserts a finger into her ass as she squeals with delight. He withdraws and the warm water makes it easy to push several fingers in at once, finger fucking her ass as she bounces up and down on his hard throbbing cock.

Just as he's about to come, he places one hand either side of her ass, lifting her up and off his cock and moves her swiftly forward just enough to push his cock gently into her ass. He holds her in place, and she moves up and down in a rhythmic motion as the tightness of her sends him spiralling out of control. The two other girls are facing each other standing over him taking it in turns to finger fuck each other while kissing erect nipples and greedily kissing each other's necks and mouths.

Once finished playing, they move him into another larger bath and take turns to wash him then leave him to wallow in a glow of total satisfaction. They dress in flowing see-through dresses and then it's back to work and off into one of the other playrooms to fuck and suck and do whatever is required of them. The opium certainly helps to takes the edge of the demands of the working day and night.

Ottis moves around the house glancing into various rooms, he likes to be a voyeur and was most impressed watching the girls in the tub.

In the purple room is an older lady wearing black stockings, no panties and a red basque pulled down exposing nipples in clamps suspended by a swing made by one of his footmen. Her feet are in straps holding her legs wide apart, leather straps across her lower back and thighs are holding her in place, her plump backside exposed, she's swinging gently being pushed back and forth by a couple of very attractive muscular young men in red and black masks, one standing behind her and one in front dressed in red leather shorts and nothing else, their cocks exposed and erect.

The one in front of her is holding an item shaped like a large fat cock and inserting it onto the opening between her legs every time the swing sways towards him. It goes in and out with ease, nice and slowly teasing her, she's gasping each time it enters her, she's begging for more, the teasing is relentless. Her wrists are bound by thick leather straps tethered to either side of the swing, now and then the man behind her tightens and releases the nipple clamps, the feeling is so exquisite she wants to explode, but the men won't let her, not yet.

Stopping the swinging motion, the man in front starts to lick and probe her wet opening, alternating with fucking her with the cold wet fucking toy, stopping just before she's about to climax, the teasing goes on and on and is relentless. Finally she's released from her anguish as she is penetrated, the one behind holds her still in the swing and positions himself so that he can fuck her ass and the other joins in from the front, removes the fucking toy and enters where the toy had been. Double penetration, exactly what the swing is designed for.

Ottis moves out of the house, there are two new wings with playrooms, a stable, bathhouses and a garden with a beautiful pathway leading to the house that has a large dining room, reception area and ten more rooms for workers and friends. He goes into the kitchen to work on the meal for tonight's guests, crab pâté starter, sweet meats with creamy mash and vegetables for main and a trifle in the shape of a woman for dessert. Ottis insisted on making the main course himself.

Tonight is somewhat of a celebration as it's a year to the day since he took over the dump and has totally transformed it. He notices carriages, the first guests are arriving. He enters the lobby of the main house, Low Lin and Sue Lin are standing beside him ready to welcome the guests' arrival. Low Lin is explaining to Sue Lin that there was an issue earlier in the bathhouse, one of the other young girls had been instructed to deal with it.

A regular, a well-known judge in the local area, had refused to bathe, a requirement before entering any playroom. On plying him with more wine he finally relented and was already in the dining room having been led there by the young girl in a knee-length white skirt with no under garments on. You could see right through it when the light hit it and a red top with white ribbons securing it instead of buttons. There were other young girls dressed the same, standing holding trays of wine ready to welcome the rest of the guests.

Placed around the table were name cards in gold for the men and silver for the women; this evening some of the guests had wives with them.

After the meal, the men were led into the card room and the ladies to various playrooms that they had already requested when booking the evening.

One requested two young men to play with, the other wanted a lady, all tastes were catered for. The judge's wife wanted a young man and girl to play with and liked to have the girl dress as a nun and have the man slap the girl's bare arse, then fuck her in front of her while she played with herself in front of them.

Another wanted a girl to dress as a school teacher and whip her backside with a cane while her husband watched and then he would fuck them both any way he pleased; this brought her no end of pleasure.

A lawyer's wife, a young pretty slip of a girl, liked to be naked and tied to the sex swing above a bed that sways back and forth.

Below her lies a naked whore being fucked by her husband who lies on top of her, every time she swings she likes to push both her feet against his backside pushing him further into her, her pointed heels marking the skin on his backside. Seeing him wince in pain gives her immense enjoyment, every now and then she cracks a whip across his naked back. Next time she must wear her riding boots with spurs.

Woods is in the pale blue room with the preacher's wife. She's teaching her how to please her husband and herself. The drugs she's taking are numbing her mind and body and she is becoming quite the actress that Ottis has required her to be.

Ottis excuses himself from the proceedings and sits in his office sipping a glass of cognac smiling to himself. He's happy with the events of the evening, everything is falling into place, boats are arriving at regular intervals supplying new girls and wine and opium on a regular basis. More money is coming in from guests than he could ever have imagined.

He leans back in his chair grinning happily at his newfound wealth. He orders a thousand sheaths as each room is going through a surprisingly high number. This time half the order will be with red ribbon ties around the tops of them and the other half with black ribbon ties, to be split between the two Diamond house playrooms.

Chapter 6

Ottis leans back in his chair in the office of the Red Diamond with a drink in his hand. There's a knock at the door. Ladyfingers, his card dealer, comes in from the card room, Ottis looks up at her. 'It's the preacher, he wants a credit of five hundred, he's playing cards with the sea captain, they've both had big losses before.'

Ottis replies, 'Let him have it, he has a boat that he won off the sea captain last time he played and lost, secure the loan against that.'

The sea captain is already beholden to Ottis owing money that he repays on a regular basis. That will be the two of them on his books now. "I wonder who will be next," he thought to himself.

He gazes out of the window as a dark cloud goes by and he thinks it's been too easy so far, acquiring properties and taking over people's lives. He has an uneasy feeling that at some point or other in the not too distant future someone is not going to be so co-operative and not take things lying down. It's not all about the money, it's about who is in charge and running things. He has to admit it's all getting a bit big for him to handle alone.

There's a boat that's late coming in, it's two weeks overdue. He's put word out about it being missing along with his latest wine order and a large stash of opium for the Red Diamond. He rings his bell for Low Lin, a letter has arrived, he reads it then hands it to her.

It's about the boat, someone has anonymously tipped him off saying it's two hundred miles away in a small harbour and is empty. Ottis looks at Low Lin and says, 'Can you get Audrey for me?'

Ottis hands the letter to her. 'Audrey, I need to leave to attend a family matter. I'll be away for two weeks or so, can you look into the missing boat issue, find out if it is our boat? Can I leave that with you?' Audrey agrees.

Ottis leaves and Audrey asks Low Lin if she will help her. Low Lin has heard that Bella, who runs the bar along the road, has heard whisperings about the missing boat and that she may know something. They agree to go the next day to speak to Bella.

Low Lin, Jade and Audrey leave for the bar the following day. They find a table in the corner and ask for Bella. A stout, well-dressed lady appears. Audrey says, 'I'm Audrey, this is Low Lin and Jade, we work for Ottis who runs the Red Diamond, one of our boats and all the crew has gone missing somewhere up the coast and it's my understanding that you may know something about it. If you do and we find it, there will be a hefty reward.' She drops a fifty-pound note on the table. 'Would this help you remember something?'

Bella replies, 'I have some men up that way that I've heard talk of the boat, the Zodiac Star. Is that the one?' Audrey confirms it is. Bella snatches the money and exclaims, 'Leave it with me and I'll get back to you. I presume I'll find you at the Red Diamond?' Audrey nods and they leave the bar.

Bella contacts Audrey to explain the exact location of the Zodiac Star and she heads up the coast with Jade and Low Lin. They board the boat at dusk and find the captain unconscious from booze. They take him down to the stern of the boat and tie him up. On waking he confesses that he had wanted to sell the wine and drugs himself and had bribed the crew to go along with his plan. He thought the boat would not be found, and half of the wine and drugs was still on board the boat.

Audrey persuades him to take the boat back and they hatch a plan to tell Ottis that the boat and crew were attacked by local smugglers and that some of the wine and drugs were stolen and that the rest was hidden and not found. In return they will spare him his life. He has seen with his own eyes what Low Lin and Jade are capable of and that they are serious with their threats; he feels he has no choice but to agree.

Two weeks later when Ottis returns, the boat is back and Audrey explains what's happened, half the wine and drugs are recovered and that the smugglers were caught and disposed of. He is so impressed and astonished with the way she's handled everything. There is a glint in her eye as she's speaking that's stirring something inside him. He finds himself staring at her and it's almost as if he's seeing her properly for the very first time.

Audrey advises that there is nothing more for Ottis to do other than go back to the Black Diamond to finish arranging the masked ball. He takes hold of her hand and exclaims, 'Audrey, I really need you to come with me to organise the ball, there is a lot to arrange and having you by my side will make it run smoothly and take the pressure off. We can leave together in four days' time.'

Audrey is stunned by the sudden rush of chemistry she's feeling as Ottis took hold of her hand, and she nods in agreement. The tip of her tongue moistens her lips as her mouth has suddenly gone dry and she finds herself unable to speak. With that she hurriedly leaves the room.

Ralph and Pierre are sitting in the Blind Duck bar next to the harbour along the road from the Red Diamond drinking beer thinking that it's not fair that their Uncle Ottis has it all. They are doing all the work bringing in the dope and booze, supplying the Red and Black Diamond and only getting a meagre wage for all the work they are doing.

They are also furious that Audrey will be leaving with Ottis and going to the Black Diamond and that she'll be helping him arrange the annual masked summer ball. Also, his announcement that she will be in charge of the distribution of alcohol and drugs to the Black and Red Diamond has them incensed with rage.

For some time they have been taking some of the dope for themselves and selling it to the locals in the pub and dealing with Jack Ice, known as the Ice Man who owns the bar. He's a giant of a man feared by most. In return he pays the boys for the drugs and his bouncer, Benny, who is a big heavy set man with the kind of face only a mother could love and with hands like hammers, distributes it for them.

Benny is not the type of man you would want to argue with, often getting into fights, and looking around the bar, there are several dents in the wall where Benny has smashed someone's head or face into it. He's feared by most of the locals and he's Ice Man's right-hand man.

In the pub there are several rooms upstairs used as a brothel, nothing as glamorous as the playrooms at the Black or Red Diamond. The pub is rough in comparison and so are most of the clientele. The boys are frequent visitors, Ralph preferring young girls and Pierre likes it rough and prefers young men, something they want to hide from Ottis.

Ralph and Pierre are being bullied by Benny to sell more and more drugs to Ice Man. The demand they realise they can't sustain long term without drawing suspicion and attention to themselves. Benny has demanded double the amount every month, meanwhile Ice Man's wife, Leslie, is not at all happy with the amount of drugs coming into the pub and decides to pay Audrey a visit, hoping she can help in some way.

Leslie is sitting in the office at the Red Diamond with Audrey and is feeling pretty uncomfortable in the plush surroundings. She's feeling hot and flustered in her heavy tweed skirt, man's shirt and heavy boots, and she can't help comparing herself to Audrey who is dressed so elegantly. Her skin is flawless and looks like fine porcelain, she has such a beautiful complexion with a slim build and the slight touch of grey in her hair really suits her and reflects her age that she thinks is similar to her own. However they are worlds apart in every way, Leslie feels very out of place and out of her depth. She can hear herself rambling on about the exploits of Ralph and Pierre, she just hopes she's making sense.

Audrey opens the door to a young girl carrying a tray of home-made cakes and tea for them both as she listens intently to Leslie. Since Audrey has been in charge of distribution of the opium to the boys, she was beginning to suspect something was amiss as the money coming in didn't seem to add up correctly. She thanks Leslie and assures her that the matter will be dealt with, and if there are any more repercussions her end, to come back and see her.

Audrey arranges for Tom, the personal coach driver for Ottis, to follow the boys each time they leave the Red Diamond and she thinks to herself that they probably think that, because of their status, even if caught they will get away with it.

Eventually Tom follows Pierre and Ralph to the pub and intercepts them before they arrive. He finds the drugs on them and explains to the boys that Audrey knows all about their exploits and if they don't stop what they are doing she will inform Ottis. No doubt they will then be thrown out onto the streets to fend for themselves as to double-cross Ottis is not something he can forgive easily.

The boys have no choice but to agree to toe the line and are told that she'll be watching them. In return she will pay for the regular visits to the pub's brothel and Ottis will be none the wiser regarding that. She knows all about their perverse behaviour and promises to keep that between themselves.

The next day Ottis and Audrey leave with coach driver Tom for the Black Diamond. Preparations need to be arranged for the annual ball, the main event of the year.

They chat excitedly on the trip back along the coast road arranging the guest list. Jason and Abbi and their two girls, Lara and Zara, are top of the list along with Mrs B and Benson and their two girls, Sue and Jackie, from Jason's household. It's a long time since they have seen them all, more than a year.

They have heard that the girls are doing well with their studies. Some of the staff are invited. Jo Jo, their housekeeper, will have the night off to attend, and of course, Patti and Sahara.

Also invited will be Tom his coachman and Low Lin and her sister Sue Lin and Jade, this year an invitation will go out to the owners of the Grand Hotel as well as some of their prestigious regular party goers.

This year Ali, Aditi, Aya, Ralph and Pierre won't be attending as they are looking after the affairs at the Red Diamond. That news no doubt won't go down very well, but the annual pay rise that's to be announced shortly for all the staff should help soften the blow.

Audrey will be at the top table this year with Patti and Sahara, Woods will not be invited, and neither will any of the other working girls. Instead some of them will be serving the food and drinks.

The menu will be discussed with his lead cook in due course. This year will be a masked event and the dress code is ballgowns for the women and evening attire for the gentlemen, the band supplying the music will be same as last year.

The invitations are sent out and distributed by Bill, and there is an air of excitement building in the Black Diamond as preparations get underway. The event is always so extravagant with no expense spared, the best wine and champagne is ordered and the ballroom decorated tastefully.

Abbi and the girls have ordered their ballgowns to be made by the tailor in the village nearby. The money she received in an envelope more than a year ago had indeed been from Ottis for her daughters and to be kept aside to buy ballgowns for them all and also to pay for their studies. The girls were so excited, as were Mrs P's daughters, Sue and Jackie. Benson had been saving hard making sure he had the money for all their new outfits. Everyone had been talking about it for weeks now and the date was fast approaching.

Chapter 7

The long sweeping driveway is lit up by lanterns and the horses and carriages are all beautifully decorated and lined up one behind the other moving forward slowly entering the grounds of the Black Diamond. The night of the masked ball has finally arrived and the bathhouse will be closed for the evening.

Footmen open the doors of the carriages and ladies in elegant ballgowns with men on their arms enter the grand house.

Standing in the entrance hall to greet each guest on their arrival is Ottis, Audrey, Patti and Sahara, all looking elegant and holding up masks decorated with jewels to match their various ballgowns.

Audrey is in a crinoline gold and black ballgown that sparkles as the light hits it, Sahara looks stunning in purple and gold that complements her beautiful dark complexion and Patti radiates sex appeal in the most exquisite shade of red and black.

The men bow and the ladies curtsy to each other on entering and are led into the drawing room where champagne and canapés are served on large silver platters.

An elegant lady sits playing a piano in the corner of the room with a string quartet. The ambience is just right, soft lighting frames the room, and all the guests chat excitedly as old friends catch up with each other and some make new acquaintances.

Every lady attending the ball has a small purse attached to her wrist or on a small belt on their dress with a dance card inside with the list of dances for the entire evening and a pencil for her to mark which dance partner and dances she will partake in. Some ladies' cards are already full while others float around the room hoping to fill up their cards before the dancing starts later in the evening.

There is an air of anticipation and excitement in the room, the single ladies hope to meet with a suitor tonight and progress to perhaps a walk on a Sunday through the park if they wish to be seen, while others hope for a drive through the park in a carriage as a way of being more discreet. That way they can sit back and not be seen at all.

As the dancing gets underway a young man in his late twenties finds himself flirting outrageously with Abbi's daughter, Lara, the champagne going to her head after one glass. He's already done his research and thinks she's a good catch.

He needs money for his wheeling and dealing and underneath his cool gentlemanly exterior lies a rogue if ever there was one. His title is easy to hide behind. He's dancing with her and she's flattered by the attention, his fingers running up and down her back discreetly when no one is looking, she's gazing up at him star struck by his good looks and charm.

The dance ends and he asks her if she has the next dance lined up, she replies that her dance card is empty for the next few dances and looks up at him full of awe and expectation. He takes her arm in his and suggests a breath of fresh air out on the veranda via the library.

Eager to please him, Lara walks with him into the library, once there he closes the door behind him, pushes her against the wall, and lifts her dress up while showering her neck gently and very slowly with kisses. She's taken by surprise and overwhelmed by his attention, she's feeling giddy with the wine and her mind is reeling with feelings she's never felt before. This man must love her, she's sure of that.

His fingers find their way up the outside of her leg to the top of her lace stocking, and just at that moment, the door bursts open and her sister Zara walks in with Jade, the two of them horrified at the sight in front of them.

Jade rushes over and grabs him by the back of the shirt collar twisting it, it's almost choking him, and drags him across the library out onto the veranda and into the garden. Lara bursts into tears sobbing as Zara comforts her.

Jade glares at him. 'A man should not drink if he cannot hold it and should certainly not push himself onto a vulnerable under age young lady, now get out of my sight.' With that the young lad, red faced, runs off across the garden towards the coach house.

Meanwhile in the ballroom on the opposite side of the dance floor guests are helping themselves to the buffet as the band takes a break. What an elegant affair. Food is plentiful and ranges from swan, salmon, duck, sliced roast pig, and beautifully created platters of vegetables and fruits.

The band on the stage is military based, they play all kinds of music and play in order to match the ladies' dance cards.

Woods is upstairs keeping the girls in order. It's a well-known fact kept between the guests downstairs that should they wish to excuse themselves from the ballroom and engage in a liaison or a flirtation, their desires will be catered for, at a price of course.

The preacher's wife, Dorina, wanders upstairs with Woods who takes her into a room and sits chatting for a while. She had requested to learn how to please her husband more, physically.

Woods says, 'I have a surprise for you.' She opens the door, and there is a man standing there. She ushers him in, and Woods leaves the room, closing the door quietly behind her.

The young man has a bottle of champagne and two glasses, he opens the bottle and pours a glass for her and half a glass for himself. Her mouth is dry with anticipation, she's wondering what comes next.

She nervously drinks the champagne quickly, he takes her glass and his and stands them on the bedside table, steps in front of her, takes her hands and helps her to stand. He runs his fingers through her hair and kisses her gently.

He moves his hands slowly down her body and starts to undress her, takes her hands and places them on the front of his shirt and moves her fingers gesturing to undo his buttons.

Both fully naked they slide into bed. He lays back and he teaches her how to put a sheath on a man and how to manoeuvre herself to slide easily onto him.

His arms go down her shoulders caressing her arms, then his thumbs play with her nipples which heightens her pleasure in a way she's never experienced before.

Sahara and Patti are in a small bathhouse in the grounds of the garden after excusing themselves. Their duty as professional aids to Ottis can sometimes take its toll on them and they decide to take some time out for themselves tonight.

No one will notice them missing for an hour or so, it's a hot clammy evening and they were glad to change out of their heavy ballgowns into ankle length skirts and white ruffle blouses. They take off the whips they have strapped to their legs that doubles up as lethal swords and lay them to one side.

In the bathhouse is a cool plunge pool next to a spa, this area is out of bounds tonight to guests, therefore, they know they will not be disturbed. The music has started up again and the second half of the dancing has recommenced.

Sahara undresses Patti slowly and the sight of her perfect white flesh always sends waves of desire through every fibre of her body. She slowly peels down the white ruffle shirt over her pert breasts to reveal pink rosebud nipples, eagerly she sucks one then the other. Patti's breath changes and she feels her heart beating faster with anticipation.

She helps her out of her ankle boots and undoes the belt of her long skirt which falls around her feet. Patti sits on the side of the cool plunge pool, the white flesh of her buttocks flinching as the cold marble reacts with the heat of her body.

Sahara runs her tongue up the outside of her thighs, slowly parting her legs. Patti throws her head back, now fully naked and panting with desire.

Sahara places her hands on either side of Patti's exquisite cheeks and draws her towards her, taking her time and kisses her, pulls away, stands up and says, 'Watch me dance and do not move.'

They can hear the music coming from the ballroom, it's almost hypnotic as Sahara runs her hands over her own body to the beat of the music. Patti can't help herself and goes to move towards her to put her hands on the back of her thighs, but she is stopped by Sahara who pushes her gently back into a seated position.

Patti sits back down, her body aching for Sahara, the dance continues as Sahara asks Patti to unzip each boot and slowly takes them off then peels of her own skirt and blouse in time to the music.

Her chocolate skin is glowing with sweat and desire as their eyes lock, her underwear is kicked to one side and Sahara. now naked. places one leg either side of Patti's breasts squeezing her thighs together and slides down her body, her thighs landing on top of Patti's.

Patti fondles and sucks each breast as Sahara reaches down in between Patti's open legs, her fingers moving in and out, they both know what they want and need. The two bodies almost melt together as one, the deep mahogany beauty merging with the white goddess as they roll into the cool water together.

Woods is gazing through the corner glass window. She's followed the girls to the summer house and it's not the first time she's been intrigued by them, her desire is mounting at the sight before her. Her secret attraction and desire for them both is something she keeps to herself in fear of being ridiculed.

Woods moves her panties to one side and starts to play with herself in unison with the girls. Her whole body is on fire as she lets out rasping gasps she's trying to suppress as she reaches a climax, fiercer than anything she's experienced with a man. Her secret desire for them both bursting from within her, it's almost too painful to bear, tears prick in her eyes as she wipes them away.

Back in the ballroom, Ottis is dancing with Audrey and he's leading her around the room with such grace.

All eyes are upon them, she is so beautiful and elegant never missing a step, and they dance together impeccably, a perfect match.

Audrey is glowing with happiness and joy, it's written all over her face. Ottis has not left her side all evening, it's obvious to all that the pair are very much in love. There is a softness to Ottis that people have noticed, the likes that they have never seen before. They don't take their eyes off each other as they glide around the ballroom.

The evening is drawing to an end as carriages draw up outside, ready to take the various guests home. Ottis is standing with Audrey smiling, happy with the evening's events. Guests come up to them on leaving, thanking them for their hospitality.

Once the last guests leave Ottis leads Audrey into the office, and closes the door. She goes to sit down in her chair and Ottis makes them a brandy and soda each. He hands her the drink as he sits in his chair next to her. The pair suddenly feel quite weary, it's been a busy evening, but everything had exceeded all their expectations.

Ottis stands and gently pulls Audrey up off her seat, takes her drink from her and places it on the desk. He pulls her towards him, holding his body against hers, looks into her eyes and without thinking, kisses her passionately, releases her and whispers into her ear, 'My darling, Audrey, you have made this evening a most memorable one, us being together feels perfect.'

The annual ball will be the talk of the town for many days to come. Ottis thinks to himself that he has never felt so happy and content as in this very moment gazing into the eyes of his beloved Audrey. He holds her hand, kisses it, and looking into her eyes, asks if she will make him the happiest man in the world and become his wife.

Audrey whispers a yes as tears form in her eyes and says, 'Ottis I would be honoured, you my love make my life so complete, this has been the best night of my life.' He stands, takes her in his arms and kisses her goodnight. She blushes and retires to her room, her head spinning from all the dancing and is completely overwhelmed by his proposal. This she thinks is a night she will never forget.

Chapter 8

In the Red Diamond, Aditi sits looking around the plush office smiling to herself feeling pleased to be in charge jointly with Ali and Aya. The three of them make an impressive team, each of them with different strengths that Ottis admires.

She's concerned about the twins, Pierre and Ralph. It's like they couldn't wait for Ottis to go back to the Black Diamond before getting into more mischief. The two of them were missing and she had sent for Jade and a new girl they've just recruited called Kitty and instructed them to find them and bring them back to her.

The Blind Duck seemed like the sensible place to start looking, no doubt they were both on the drink and drugs again.

The girl behind the bar tries to be clever saying she hasn't seen them, but Kitty, who is a bit of a rough diamond, her husband was in the army and she's had a bit of a hard life, starts arguing with her, picks up a pint ordered by someone else, swallows it in one go, slams it back onto the bar top, and says, 'Do you like your white teeth or do you want to lose them?'

The barmaid just stares at her not replying, so Kitty bellows, 'Tell me where Pierre and Ralph are now.' Kitty stands five foot ten inches tall and dresses like a man, has a rough voice that is anything but feminine and the barmaid realises she is not the type of person to argue with. She points to the corner of the bar.

Ralph is lying unconscious on the floor. Kitty marches over, grabs another half-finished pint from a table and pours it over Ralph. As he comes to spluttering, she grabs him by the scruff of his neck and throws him into the street. Kitty looks at Jade and says, 'Keep an eye on him will you while I find out where Pierre is.'

Ralph lies there making no attempt to move. Jade kicks him a couple of times and demands he gets to his feet, she doesn't want him falling unconscious again.

A few minutes later Kitty appears with Pierre wearing just his underpants. She found him upstairs in between two whores on a bed with his pants round his ankles, all three dead to the world, unconscious with booze. She soon woke him up throwing a barrel of urine she'd found in the corner of the room over the three of them.

The two boys are marched back to the Red Diamond, red faced and ashamed of their filthy appearance and lack of clothes. The girls take them to the bathhouse, dump them into a cold bath, give them a bar of soap and tell them to scrub themselves clean or they will be back to scrub them with a yard brush.

Tom appears with two buckets of hot water, feeling sorry for them, so they leave them with Tom to supervise, returning later. They then march them down to the cellar where there are two matrasses on the floor, a pile of blankets and some old clothes.

Kitty turns to them and says, 'Right, this is where you will stay until you both sober up, in the corner are several barrels of white wash, your job is to stay in this room while you wash all the walls, your meals will be brought to you.'

Ralph takes a blanket and curls up in the corner, his back to the room, depression washing over him. He hasn't the energy to do anything or to argue.

Pierre staggers towards Kitty yelling at her, she gives him a back handed slap that knocks him sideways sprawling him onto the floor. Kitty and Jade leave, locking them in.

The instructions from Audrey and Ottis are that they have to no longer be supported in anyway due to their behaviour, the disappearing for days on end was becoming a regular occurrence, surely they didn't think it would continue to go unnoticed.

Audrey instructed Jade to stop all payments to them and the regular payment to the Blind Duck was also to stop forthwith.

Three months later Ralph is clean and has moved back into his old room in the Red Diamond. He's in the bathhouse to have a wash and shave from one of the girls working there when the door opposite opens midway through his shave.

Ralph is sat in the bath with a cloth over his face, therefore, he can't see who it is. Someone starts washing him, he moves the cloth from his face, it's a young lass, Belinda, that he's been seeing for some time now. The shave finished, he ushers the working girl out of the room, pulls Belinda into the bath with him as she giggles.

Water going everywhere, she straddles him, her white dress riding up exposing her bare legs, and to his surprise, no panties. She bends down to kiss him and the passion ignites inside them both as he eases himself gently inside her, the warm water flowing around them. The love he feels for this woman is undeniable, the secret they have kept for so long has to be out in the open as of now. The decision made by them both is to explain everything to Ottis and Audrey.

They get dried and she agrees to leave with him in the next few days to explain their plans to Ottis. Her family own a coach house and he wants to take it on with her and in return promises to stay off the drink and drugs if they will help him and release him from the Red Diamond.

He needs money to renovate the coach house that is twenty miles from the Red Diamond in the direction of the Black Diamond, therefore, in the perfect location. He suggests that Tom and himself run it together as Tom has experience in that field.

He hopes to then run a fleet of coaches with horses that would go up and down the coast from one house to the other. Then there is the other matter of the child they have together that they have kept secret, no more lies and no more secrets from now on.

Ralph speaks to Audrey and Ottis and is delighted with the outcome, they are behind him with his new plans and lend him the money he needs. They will all work together on the coach house project with Belinda's mother, her father having died in the war. Tom knew her late father, he was a fine upstanding man well thought of.

The coach house has been neglected since losing her father; it's been a real struggle to keep things going. The six rooms have not been let for some time and are in desperate need of renovation.

Ottis can see the potential of helping Ralph and Tom being on board. Working in unison with Ralph is an excellent idea as all the coach drivers in the area know Tom and he's highly respected. The project can't fail, it's win, win for them all and will bring more clients to the Black and Red Diamonds.

Pierre on the other hand has managed to convince everyone that he's staying on the straight and narrow and has always been jealous of Ralph. It's been bubbling away under his cool exterior for quite some time, and his obsession to have sex with random men and women and not being able to stop is taking its toll on him.

So far, he's managed to hide his drinking and still function and he's cleverly stealing whatever he can from the Red Diamond, the odd trinket here and there and selling things on. He's not making enough to buy drugs and is having to make do with drink instead. His habit is becoming worse and worse as he needs more and more alcohol just to get through the day.

He's now having sex with various men and women and charging for it, the alcohol helps numb his mind, he's not sleeping, and alcohol helps him sleep.

He feels it's a vicious circle that he just can't seem to break and get away from. He feels it's so unfair, why should Ralph be so happy suddenly and seems to have turned his life around so quickly. He feels left on the scrap heap, hating himself. They are no longer on speaking terms, he misses his brother and has found himself feeling totally lost and alone.

He's now living in a cave near the Red Diamond with like-minded lost souls stealing what he can and bringing the goods back to the cave to pass on to the runners who sell the various items, and in return, he's getting the alcohol that his body and mind is craving.

Two men had paid him a visit earlier in the day and explained that there is an establishment nearby called The Boar's Head. It was previously a small coach house and now all run-down and the owner is a vicious bully who is with a woman and her two nephews, all three of them working there under duress. The bully is the woman's ex-husband's brother, her husband died and rumour has it that the brother killed him.

They explain that they see it as an opportunity to take it over if they can get rid of the brother. The woman approached them, begging for help asking if they can dispose of him and set her free from all the abuse and bullying.

All three see this as an opportunity to turn it into a bar and use it for their alcohol and drug business, a step up from operating from a cave, that's for sure, and a business venture they can share.

Pierre is already regularly visiting the opium den behind the Red Diamond and stealing what drugs he can. Ottis seems to have taken his eye of the ball since being so infatuated with Audrey and that's working in his favour.

He could have his own little empire very soon, and the three men formulate a plan to visit the coach house as soon as possible. He's not feeling too good, too much alcohol and drugs in his system, he can't seem to think straight and knows he's in no fit state to go with them. He tells them to dispose of the bully boy themselves and let him know when that's done.

Days and nights seem to blur together for Pierre, he's often not sure what is actual reality or made up in his mind. The visit from the two men. Did he make that up as there has been no sign of them for what seems like several days.

Events turn from bad to worse. He's curled up in a ball in the corner of the cave replaying last night's events although they are blurred round the edges. He remembers being in one of the bedrooms of the Red Diamond when a girl comes in and catches him stealing some jewellery he's found in a bedside drawer.

Is all very hazy and he's trying to figure out if it's just his mind playing tricks on him. He belted her across the face, she fell against some bedroom furniture, and split her head open as she hit her head on the corner of the unit.

She was so light to carry, he bundled her up in a blanket and carried her outside, dumped her in the pigsty down the road and disposed of her clothes.

There must have been blood on the carpet in the bedroom, he's shaking trying to piece it all together. Who was the girl? He's not sure, not someone he's seen before, what little peace of mind he had, and it wasn't much, is now in turmoil with the realisation that he's perhaps killed an innocent girl. What sort of monster had he become? Self-loathing washes over him and an alcohol-fuelled sleep, finally gives him some peace.

Another terror filled dream, this time it's the men that visited several days previously. He's with them in the coach house. There is shouting and screaming, a fat oaf of a man on top of a woman, he can see the helpless look in her eye begging them to help her. Then there is the blood, he's killed him, stabbed him in the back relentlessly with a knife. Dream or reality, he has no idea. Then blackness and peace finally washes over him again but not for long as the nightmares return, replaying over and over again, torturing and tormenting him.

Chapter 9

Pierre opens his eyes and there's an angel looking at him. No wait, it's the woman in his dream. Is he still dreaming? He tries to speak and no words come, she lifts a cup of water to his mouth, and he drinks gratefully.

He looks around and does not recognise his surroundings. He's in a bed in a room he's not seen before. Confused he looks at her, she's full of concern and the kind warm look on her face overwhelms him and brings tears to his eyes.

She says, 'I'm Emily, you are going to be OK, thank you for helping me, I am finally free. This is all yours now, I am going to help you get better.' Still confused, Pierre drifts of to sleep.

Emily looks after Pierre for several weeks, nursing him back to health. No one has come looking for him from the Red Diamond, they have all washed their hands of him quite some time ago.

He learns that his nightmare was in fact in part reality, someone had killed the bully that had been abusing her for years since her husband died, however, no one is sure who it was. She is assuming it was him, however, she wasn't there despite his nightmare of her being there. He was found unconscious by her at the scene of the crime.

Over time, he finds himself falling for her. Her two grown-up nephews, however, are not happy with the situation, something he felt he would work on and hopefully win them over given time.

He decided he would make something of himself, turn his life around like his brother, live with Emily for a while and then approach his family hoping that they will forgive and forget the past.

Several months pass by and Audrey hears that Pierre has successfully taken charge of the Boar's Head and has met up with him several times and finds herself rather taken with Emily and the way Pierre has handled things. Having a good caring woman in tow seems to be agreeing with him and helping him to settle down. She's concerned that the police are clamping down on opium dens, and on discussing things further with Ottis, they agree to hand over that side of the business to Pierre, he can run everything out of the Boar's Head.

Arrangements are made and plans bought into fruition to turn the opium den and cottages behind the Red Diamond into more rooms so that they can hire new oriental girls from various other countries.

Pierre is happy that he's back in with his family, however, Emily's nephews, Jonathan and Kristopher, are riddled with jealousy of the new endeavour. They begin scheming, ideally they want rid of Pierre, as they believe they can run things perfectly well without him, Emily has a good head for business and they don't think they need him around ordering them about.

Jonathan and Kristopher are like their father in nature, mid-twenties, three years in age apart, self-centred, good looking young men, both just over six feet in height, well built with good physiques, spoilt really over the years and always get what they want.

Both petty thieves all their lives, they have grown up watching their father abuse their mother then their aunt and they too walk all over her and any woman they meet. They are always trying to outdo each other, both with egos so large, unable to control the rages that burn inside themselves.

Pierre now in tow with their aunt has put a stop to any bullying, they feel pushed to one side and no longer in control. Both have several children and no fixed partner and perhaps some children they don't even know about. They have drifted through life using and abusing any woman that comes their way, picking women that are weak willed and broken, charming their way through life, leaving a trail of broken hearts and shattered dreams behind them.

A plan is formulated in the boys' minds. They make a mental note that Pierre has a routine of taking himself off to bed on his own for a few hours on certain evenings.

On one such occasion, both high on drugs, they creep into their mother's bedroom to find Pierre indeed alone and asleep. Kristopher pushes him onto his front and holds him there while Jonathan tries to suffocate him with a pillow holding it over his face.

He's no right to come in and take over, they want back what is theirs. When done with him, they will teach their aunt a lesson. Pierre struggles managing to push Jonathan off him, he releases the pillow and Pierre gasps for air, raises his arms up to defend himself as Kristopher slashes him across his arm with a knife.

Emily hears yelling from downstairs and comes rushing into the bedroom, startling the boys who back off and make a run for it, pushing past her and knocking her down.

They stumble downstairs into the main bar, blood on their clothes and rush over to the bar area opening a drawer where the takings are kept, grab all the notes and rush out of the main door.

Emily is at the top of the stairs screaming for someone to get a doctor. One of the locals suggests they take him there and several of the men help carry him down the stairs, his arm wrapped in a sheet.

The outcome is severe nerve damage and it's unlikely he will ever be able to use that arm properly again, however, he's grateful just to be alive as he saw the fury and hatred in the boys' eyes that night and is sure they were hoping to kill him.

Emily has been used and abused by men all her life, including her two nephews who she wished had never been born. Pure evil that's all they were. She knew that it would be most unlikely that they would show up again as they were now wanted men and all the regulars in the bar were witnesses to what happened, and if seen, they would be turned over to the press gangs.

Over time, Pierre and Emily came to an understanding to live together as man and wife. Slowly he was making her realise that there are good, kind men in the world, and as a woman, she felt safe, protected and valued.

Chapter 10

Life for Lara is on the up since the ball. She's been making her own clothes for herself and various friends for years as a hobby, and rather taken by the various ballgowns, decides to make some from her own designs.

With the help of Abbi and Jason, she's opened her own shop and a small factory; all the staff are on good wages and treated really well.

Her reputation has grown from strength to strength, older more affluent ladies have been approaching her and asking her to make ballgowns and formal wear for them. Girls her age were also asking her to make clothes for them rather than getting them made by tailors that their mothers chose. They find her designs more attractive, modern and up and coming for their age group.

The Grand Hotel's coffee shop being one of her favourite haunts, she likes to go there on her own and read up on the stock market and also pass the time working on her designs, taking her sketch book with her because it's not far from her shop.

The waitress that the other staff seemed to snub on her visit a few years ago when she accompanied her sister and the cook's daughters had caught her attention.

She could not help but notice that her colleagues still seemed to be bullying her, perhaps due to the fact that she did not conform to what they considered a waitress at the rather posh Grand Hotel should look like. Lara, however, saw through the plump exterior and could see an inner beauty in the girl. The others always sent her over to serve her.

Lara had learnt that her name was Rose and she had approached her some time ago in the ladies' room and handed her a beautifully wrapped bar of lavender soap and complimented her on her appearance and asked her where she had bought her dress.

Over time they had got to know each other and Lara spotted something rather unique in her, an interest in clothes and fashion and a burning desire that she recognised in herself. She asked her to come and work for her in her shop, a decision that turned out to be the right one as she now manages and brings in all the new materials and designs from France, Spain and Italy.

The look on her colleagues' faces was priceless the day she walked out. They all stood there aghast, jealously and shock on all their faces. They had all got what they deserved, left behind earning a meagre wage while Rose would be moving on to build a fashion empire with Lara, owning her own home and horse and carriage. She was the envy of many. Lara made sure she was there that day with Rose to see the look on their faces.

Ottis had thought that they would train the girls to be croupiers, however, their interests had gone in other directions and because of their close relationship with their grandparents and Jason, their influence had sent them in another direction, something Jason and Abbi were both proud and delighted about. Their grandmother had always been creative and made her own clothes when she was young, her influence had rubbed off on Lara, and her grandmother helped her set up her first shop and they were about to open a second that Rose will run.

Lara is now living in her own townhouse close to the shop, Zara is living with her grandparents in their country estate so that she can be part of that community. If she needs advice at all she often consults her sister, Lara, who has always been the sensible one and she likes to run everything by her first. The two are still close sisters and see each other as often as they can.

They may be twins, however, they have a completely different way of looking at the world.

Zara is also doing very well for herself. Her interest in horses grabbed the attention of her grandfather who had given her a horse that she dedicated all her time and attention to. She entered him into his first race and won and that was that, she got the bug and named the horse after her grandfather. He, in turn, has named his favourite horse after her.

The two of them travelled all over the country competing. She works at her grandfather's stables and buys and sells racehorses; the business will be passed to her in due course once she's learnt all there is to know.

News of the engagement between Audrey and Ottis is the talk of the town. Audrey asks Lara to design her wedding dress and the two meet up to discuss the style and there will be two bridesmaids, Lara and Zara. The two girls are over the moon and Lara also gets to work designing the bridesmaids' dresses.

The ceremony will be in the Black Diamond on the stage area and there will, of course be a wedding feast afterwards followed by an elaborate ball to celebrate the union.

Ottis and Audrey will spend a couple of hours at the ball and then Ottis will be surprising his new bride with a cruise around the Mediterranean for a fortnight, stopping off to meet some of his family as they are Sicilian. One week of luxury cruising before they reach their destination stopping off at a couple of places of interest en route.

He has booked the honeymoon suite comprising of a four-poster bed with a beautiful white cotton embroidered bedspread in a mahogany cabin on one of the upper deck areas with their own private balcony. They will also have their own personal valet and lady's maid.

Quite a lot of organizing has to be done, he needs to make sure everything is packed without Audrey knowing otherwise it will spoil the surprise. Patti and Sahara have all that in hand and will take care of the packing while Ottis is at the ball with Audrey.

The date is set for the wedding and the invitations sent out. Audrey just cannot wait to become his bride, but there is a slight niggle in the back of her mind. Her sister Woods is not invited and she can't help but think that perhaps she has paid her dues and should be freed from the slavery that holds her, working for clients day in and day out.

She doesn't really see or speak to her sister any more and hasn't seen her for such a long time. She feels too much time has passed and she really wouldn't know what to say to her. Perhaps she will talk to Ottis after the wedding and ask for her to be redeployed, to perhaps move into a better position in the household, what she has to endure now is so gruelling, and such a demoralizing role. With that in mind she pushes all thoughts of her sister to the back of her mind.

The big day arrives and everything runs smoothly for the couple, there are about half the number of guests compared to the summer ball, in fact Audrey thinks just the right number. It's a glorious day and the sun is shining, the meal planned is similar to the ball apart from the wedding cake of course. The ceremony goes smoothly and Ottis makes a heart-warming speech that has Audrey close to tears.

Audrey's dress is absolutely exquisite and everyone is talking about it. Lara will no doubt be even more inundated with orders as her designs are becoming more and more popular.

It's time to tell Audrey that they are leaving and Ottis takes her aside, and holding her hand, looks longingly into her eyes and explains that there is a surprise awaiting and that a horse and carriage is ready for their departure. Audrey asks, 'Where are we going?'

He replies, 'All in good time, my darling, come with me.'

They step into the carriage after saying their goodbyes, and the wedding party congregate outside to bid them farewell. Audrey is overcome with emotion, however, she wishes her sister was there too and regrets not speaking to Ottis about her sooner.

This truly is the most amazing and happiest day of her life, although she feels slightly nervous as the wedding night is approaching and she's never been with a man before. The champagne she hopes will help calm her nerves.

On arrival at the dock there is the captain and staff lined up alongside the ship to congratulate them on their union. Audrey is overwhelmed with excitement on seeing the size of the ship, they board and are escorted to their luxury cabin.

Audrey is delighted to see all her clothes hanging up in mahogany wardrobes and all the items she would require unpacked and in their place. He turns to her and pops open another bottle of champagne that is sat in an ice bucket next to the most exquisite bouquet of flowers.

He pours one for himself and Audrey as he makes a toast to a very happy future together. A gorgeous gold dress is laid out on the bed for her to change into later.

They sit together for a while on the balcony enjoying the perfect sunset and chatting about the day's events and how perfect it all was.

Ottis turns to Audrey and says he's going up to the top deck communal balcony to have a smoke and will leave her to change into the dress before going for dinner once the ship departs. He says he won't be long and will give her half an hour or so to freshen up and then he will be back.

On the top deck it's very quiet as the sun has gone down and the ship is not due to leave for another hour or so, as not all the guests are on board yet.

Ottis is leaning on the rails enjoying a smoke and looking out to sea, the stars are beginning to come out. Just beautiful, this really is the most perfect day and he can't wait to get back to Audrey and to later consummate their marriage. He's waited so long for her being the perfect gentleman, wanting to make their wedding night one she will never forget.

He's about to leave when he hears someone approaching. He turns slowly to see a rather beautiful, elegant lady wearing a rather striking long cape, walking slowly towards him with a silk scarf round her head that's blowing slightly in the wind across her face. There's something majestic and regal about the way she is carrying herself, confidence radiating from her.

He turns back to look up at the stars, she stands to join him and purrs, 'What a beautiful evening, I just needed some air, could I perhaps join you. Would you by any chance have a smoke?'

He glances sideways, admiring the beauty before him and without thinking finds himself replying, 'I was just about to leave to go back to my cabin, isn't it a beautiful evening, however, I'll stay a bit longer.' He hands her a tin of handmade cigarettes, and as he does so, she knocks it out of his hand with such force that it makes him jump, and the contents spill all over the deck.

He goes to pick it up, thinking she knocked it by mistake, and as he does so, she hits him on the side of the head with a heavy metal object she was hiding and sends him crashing into the railing. With all the strength she can muster, she pushes him up and over the side of the ship. As she does so his eyes open briefly, and everything seems to be moving in slow motion.

He grabs at the handrail as he falls. She removes her headscarf, and despite her make-up being cleverly done so as to disguise her appearance, recognition suddenly flickers through his mind as he exclaims, "Woods what are you doing? please help me."

Hatred and years of pent-up fury coursing through her veins, she glares at him and whispers, 'This is for all you have done to me, it's what you and my sister deserve, good bye Ottis.' She prises his fingers off the handrail so that he loses his grip and falls into the dark water below. He looks up at her as he does so, a look of complete disbelief and despair on his face. She just looks at him with no emotion on her face, throws the heavy object into the cold dark water and watches as he disappears under the waves.

With that Woods calmly turns, puts on her headscarf, holds her head up high and walks slowly and calmly off the ship without anyone noticing.

There is a bench nearby. It's quiet on the dock, no one else is around, all the guests have boarded, and she sits and glances up, recognising the figure standing on a balcony alone in a gold dress with a glass in her hand looking wistfully out to sea.

Woods smiles, finally feeling at peace as the ship's whistle blows, and as it starts to slowly make its departure from the harbour, she could swear that she saw the woman glance her way. She stands as if in slow motion, her head held high and purposely stares at the woman who is now looking in her direction, She turns very slowly to walk away and does not look back.